To my love, Ken

The
Love

A GROUNDWOOD BOOK
HOUSE OF ANANSI PRESS

of Two Stars

A KOREAN FOLKTALE RETOLD AND ILLUSTRATED BY

Janie Jaebyun Park

This is a retelling of an ancient Korean legend about two stars, Altair and Vega, or Kyonu and Jingnyo, as they are known in Korea. They meet in the Milky Way on the seventh day of the seventh month of the lunar year. A lunar year is divided into twelve lunar months. In each month the moon makes a complete revolution of the earth. In Asian-Pacific countries such as China, Japan and Korea, people hold an annual event to celebrate the love of these two stars.

I first heard the story of Kyonu and Jingnyo when I was a little girl. One summer day my grandmother and I were looking out at the rain in our garden. She told me that the raindrops were Kyonu and Jingnyo's tears. Then she told me the story you are about to read. In some versions of the tale, Kyonu and Jingnyo are a prince and princess, but this retelling is very close to the traditional version most often told. — *Janie Jaehyun Park*

Once upon a time there was a
kingdom in the starry sky.

In that realm there lived a young man, Kyonu, who was a farmer. Ever since he was a little boy, he had loved animals. Because he took such good care of them, his steers were the strongest beasts of burden in the land.

Nearby there lived a young woman named Jingnyo, who was a weaver. Because she made the most beautiful and durable cloth in the kingdom, her fabric was the most sought after, and she was kept busy at her loom day and night.

One fine day Kyonu and Jingnyo met by chance in a garden blooming with every kind of flower. They fell in love the instant they saw each other.

From that day forth their only desire was to be together. They lost all interest in their former lives. Kyonu's cattle grew sick, and Jingnyo's loom grew dusty, as they spent their days talking in the garden, reveling in their love for each other.

Meanwhile the farms in the kingdom soon became barren, as there were no more strong cattle to plow the fields. People began to grow hungry.

And their clothes began to wear thin and had to be patched, since there was no longer any fine, strong cloth to buy.

The king of the starry realm became angry with Kyonu and Jingnyo for their idleness, and he decided to separate the lovers. He sent Kyonu to the End of the East, and Jingnyo to the End of the West. But to make their separation more bearable, he told them they could meet in the Milky Way once a year, on the seventh day of the seventh moon month.

Once Kyonu and Jingnyo were separated, they sadly went back to their duties. But their hearts were broken, and they longed for each other.

Finally the seventh day of the seventh moon month came around. Kyonu and Jingnyo rushed to meet each other in the Milky Way. But the river of stars was too wide and too deep for them to get across. There was no boat to carry them and no bridge for them to walk over. They called to each other, sobbing and crying in their desperation.

Their tears flooded the earth. As the waters rose, all the beasts and birds gathered together to see if they could make this rain of tears stop. The magpies and crows thought they knew a way to help the lovers.

They flew in their thousands up into the sky. Beak to tail, wing tip to wing tip, they hovered so close together that they formed a bridge across the Milky Way. Kyonu and Jingnyo rushed to one another and embraced joyously.

When the time came to say goodbye, the lovers shed tears once again. But these tears were gentle, and when they fell on the earth, the plants flourished and bore many rich fruits.

Since that time, it is said that on the seventh day of the seventh moon month, it always rains. Kyonu and Jingnyo are crying because they must part. But fruits and vegetables grow abundantly in that soft rain. And in that season, magpies and crows go bald because Kyonu and Jingnyo have been stepping on their heads.

Text and illustrations copyright © 2005 by Janie Jaehyun Park

No part of this publication may be reproduced, stored in a retrieval system or transmitted, in any form or by any means, without the prior written consent of the publisher or a licence from The Canadian Copyright Licensing Agency (Access Copyright). For an Access Copyright licence, visit www.accesscopyright.ca or call toll free to 1-800-893-5777.

Groundwood Books / House of Anansi Press
720 Bathurst Street, Suite 500, Toronto, Ontario M5S 2R4
Distributed in the USA by Publishers Group West
1700 Fourth Street, Berkeley, CA 94710

We acknowledge for their financial support of our publishing program the Canada Council for the Arts, the Government of Canada through the Book Publishing Industry Development Program (BPIDP) and the Ontario Arts Council.

Library and Archives Canada Cataloguing in Publication
Park, Janie Jaehyun
The love of two stars : a Korean legend / retold and illustrated by Janie Jaehyun Park.
ISBN 0-88899-672-1
I. Title.
PS8581.A7558L69 2005   jC813'.6   C2004-907351-6

The illustrations are in acrylics on gessoed paper.

Printed and bound in China

40 YEARS 40 ANS

ONTARIO ARTS COUNCIL
CONSEIL DES ARTS DE L'ONTARIO